GORDON, THE BIG ENGINE

by

The Rev. W. Awdry

Grolier

Leaves

Two men were cleaning Gordon.

"Mind my eye," Gordon grumbled.

"Shut it, silly! Did ever you see such mud, Bert?"

"No I never, Alf! You ought to be ashamed, Gordon, giving us extra work."

The hosing and scrubbing stopped. Gordon opened one eye, but shut it quickly.

"Wake up, Gordon," said the Fat Controller sternly, "and listen to me. You will pull no more coaches till you are a Really Useful Engine."

So Gordon had to spend his time pulling trucks.

"Goods trains, Goods trains," he muttered. He felt his position deeply.

"That's for you!—and *you!*—*and* you!" Gordon said crossly.

"Oh! Oh! Oh! Oh!" screamed the trucks as he shunted them about the yard.

"Trucks will be trucks," said James, watching him.

"They won't with *me!*" snorted Gordon. "I'll teach them. Go on!" and another truck scurried away.

"They tried to push me down the hill this morning," Gordon explained. "It's slippery there. You'll probably need some help."

"*I* don't need help on hills," said James huffily.

Gordon laughed, and got ready for his next train.

James went away to take the Express.

"Slippery hills indeed," he snorted. "*I* don't need help."

"Come on! Come on!" he puffed.

"All in good time, all in good time," grumbled the coaches.

The train was soon running nicely, but a "Distant" signal checked them close to Gordon's Hill.

Gordon's Hill used to be bleak and bare. Strong winds from the sea made it hard to

climb. Trees were planted to give shelter, and in summer the trains run through a leafy avenue.

Now Autumn had come, and dead leaves fell. The wind usually puffed them away, but today rain made them heavy, and they did not move.

The "Home" signal showed "clear", and James began to go faster.

He started to climb the hill.

"I'll do it! I'll do it!" he puffed confidently.

Half-way up he was not so sure! "I *must* do it, I *must* do it," he panted desperately, but try as he would, his wheels slipped on the leaves, and he couldn't pull the train at all.

"Whatsthematter? Whatsthematter?" he gasped.

"Steady old boy, steady," soothed his driver.

His fireman put sand on the rails to help him grip; but James's wheels spun so fast that they only ground the sand and leaves to slippery mud, making things worse than before.

The train slowly stopped. Then—

"Help! Help! Help!" whistled James; for though his wheels were turning forwards, the heavy coaches pulled him backwards, and the whole train started slipping down the hill.

His driver shut off steam, carefully put on the brakes, and skilfully stopped the train.

"Whew!" he sat down and mopped his face. "I've never known *that* happen before."

"I have," said the fireman, "in Bincombe tunnel—Southern Region."

The guard poked his head in the cab. "Now what?" he asked.

"Back to the station," said the fireman, taking charge, "and send for a 'Banker'."

So the guard warned the signalman, and they brought the train safely down.

But Gordon, who had followed with a goods train, saw what had happened.

Gordon left his trucks, and crossed over to James.

"I thought you could climb hills," he chuckled.

James didn't answer; he had no steam!

"Ah well! We live and learn," said Gordon, "we live and learn. Never mind, little James," he went on kindly, "I'm going to push behind. Whistle when you're ready."

James waited till he had plenty of steam, then "Peep! Peep!" he called.

"Poop! Poop! Poop!"

"Pull hard," puffed Gordon.

"We'll do it!" puffed James.

"Pull hard! We'll do it," the engines puffed together.

Clouds of smoke and steam towered from the snorting engines as they struggled up the hill.

"We *can* do it!" puffed James.

"We *will* do it!" puffed Gordon.

The greasy rails sometimes made Gordon's wheels slip, but he never gave up, and presently they reached the top.

"We've done it! We've done it!" they puffed.

Gordon stopped. "Poop! Poop!" he whistled. "Goodbye."

"Peep! Peep! Peep! Peep! Thank you! Goodbye," answered James. Gordon watched the coaches wistfully till they were out of sight; then slowly he trundled back to his waiting trucks.

Paint Pots and Queens

THE stations on the Line were being painted.

The engines were surprised.

"The Queen is coming," said the painters. The engines in their shed were excited and wondered who would pull the Royal Train.

"I'm too old to pull important trains," said Edward sadly.

"I'm in disgrace," Gordon said gloomily. "The Fat Controller would never choose me."

"He'll choose me, of course," boasted James the Red Engine.

"You!" Henry snorted, "*You* can't climb hills. He will ask *me* to pull it, *and* I'll have a new coat of paint. You wait and see."

The days passed. Henry puffed about proudly, quite sure that he would be the Royal Engine.

One day when it rained, his driver and fireman stretched a tarpaulin from the cab to the tender, to keep themselves dry.

Henry puffed into the big station. A painter was climbing a ladder above the line. Henry's smoke puffed upwards; it was thick and black. The painter choked and couldn't see. He missed his footing on the ladder, dropped his paint pot, and fell plop on to Henry's tarpaulin.

The paint poured over Henry's boiler, and

trickled down each side. The paint pot perched on his dome.

The painter clambered down and shook his brush at Henry.

"You spoil my clean paint with your dirty smoke," he said, "and then you take the whole lot, and make me go and fetch some more." He stumped crossly away.

The Fat Controller pushed through the crowd.

"You look like an iced cake, Henry," he said. "*That* won't do for the Royal Train. I must make other arrangements."

He walked over to the yard.

Gordon and Thomas saw him coming, and both began to speak.

"Please Sir . . ."

"One at a time," smiled the Fat Controller. "Yes Gordon?"

"May Thomas have his Branch Line again?"

"Hm," said the Fat Controller, "well Thomas?"

"Please, Sir, can Gordon pull coaches now?"

The Fat Controller pondered.

"Hm . . . you've both been quite good lately, and you deserve a treat . . . When the Queen comes, Edward will go in front and clear the line, Thomas will look after the coaches, and Gordon . . . will pull the train."

"Ooooh Sir!" said the engines happily.

The great day came. Percy, Toby, Henry and James worked hard bringing people to town.

Thomas sorted all their coaches in the yard.

"Peep! Peep! Peep! They're coming!" Edward steamed in, looking smart with flags and bright paint.

Two minutes passed—five—seven—ten. "Poop! Poop!" Everyone knew that whistle, and a mighty cheer went up as the Queen's train glided into the station.

Gordon was spotless, and his brass shone. Like Edward, he was decorated with flags, but on his buffer beam he proudly carried the Royal Arms.

The Queen was met by the Fat Controller, and before doing anything else, she thanked him for their splendid run.

"Not at all, Your Majesty," he said, "thank *you*."

"We have read," said the Queen to the Fat Controller, "a great deal about your engines. May we see them please?"

So he led the way to where all the engines were waiting.

"Peep! Peep!" whistled Toby and Percy, "they're coming!"

"Sh Sh! Sh Sh!" hissed Henry and James.

But Toby and Percy were too excited to care.

The Fat Controller told the Queen their names, and she talked to each engine. Then she turned to go.

Percy bubbled over, "Three cheers for the Queen!" he called.

"Peeeep! Peeeep! Peeeep!" whistled all the engines.

The Fat Controller held his ears, but the Queen, smiling, waved to the engines till she passed the gate.

Next day the Queen spoke specially to Thomas, who fetched her coaches, and to Edward and Gordon who took her away; and no engines ever felt prouder than Thomas, and Edward, and Gordon the Big Engine.

This book club edition published by Grolier 1994

Published by arrangement with Reed Children's Books
First published in Great Britain 1953 as part of *The Railway Series* No. 8.
Copyright © William Heinemann Ltd. 1953.
This edition copyright © William Heinemann Ltd. 1994